Chiharu and the Magic Toothbrush

Joana Jehu-Appiah

Illustrated by Elif Esen Gökçe

and Naya Kirichenko

ISBN: 978-1-8383271-0-1

DEDICATION

To my parents - Cynthia and Jerisdan, my *biological* sisters - Sarie, Marie and Deborah, my *sociological* sisters - Sabrina (aka @mummamrsandme) Lina, Natasha, Chinma, Tracey and Hannah and my brother in law - Darren - Thank you for the continued love and support.

To my cousin - Laurina Austin Seade – Thank you for striving to push my books further afield.

To my nieces, nephews and godchildren - You inspire me to write – Thank you.

And last but certainly not least - Kana Sato and family. Thank you for your time, knowledge, availability and support, not just with this book but during my time in Japan. Without you – my experience of Japan would have been limited, and this story would not have been told.

Domo Arigatou Gozaimashita.

CONTENTS

GLOSSARY OF TERMS

Casual/informal way to address a family member from the formal term "san" (chan)

Grandfather	(ojiisan)
Grandmother	(obaasan)
Father	(otousan)
Mother	(okaasan)
Good morning	(ohayou)
Invitation to eat	(Itadakimasu)
Hot springs	(onsen)
Park	(koen)

Obon	(Ancestor's remembrance festival)
Awa Odori	(Largest dance festival in Japan)

CHAPTER 1
A Welcomed Gift

“This is for you.” Yoko handed her daughter a small box. It was carefully wrapped and decorated with a silver ribbon.

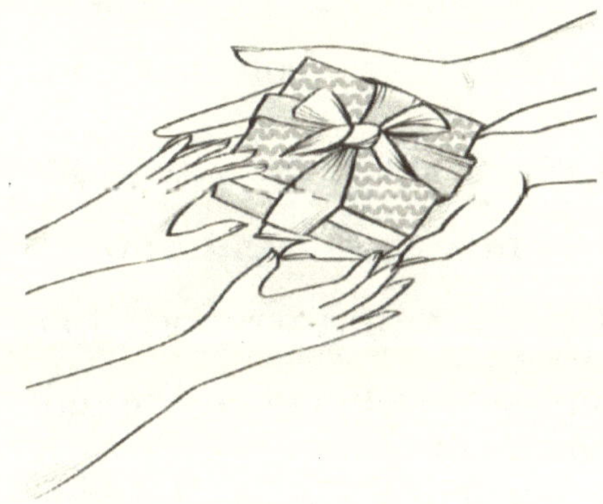

“I got it in the sales at work.”

Chiharu beamed. She had an idea what it might be. She took the box and tore the wrapper from the package carelessly. Yoko began to frown as she watched her hard work destroyed in a matter of seconds.

“Oh, okaasan!” she cried, “I love it.” She pulled the object from the box excitedly.

"Let me help you put it on." Yoko placed the item around her daughter's tiny wrist and adjusted the straps to fit comfortably. "Now you have your very own watch - be sure not to get it wet."

"I won't okaasan - I promise." Chiharu leaned forward and gave her mother a warm hug. She held her wrist up and admired the bright yellow watch. It was her favourite colour.

"It's nice to see a smile back on your face." Yoko reached into a different shopping bag and brought out another wrapped item from the department store where she worked.

"I got this for obaachan."

"What is it?" Chiharu asked.

"You'll have to wait until we see her-"

"But I want to see it now!"

Yoko looked at Chiharu disapprovingly until she lightened up. She reached into another bag and brought out a collection of clunky tools.

"Oh, obaachan will love this!"

They laughed.

Once a year, Chiharu and her mother Yoko visit obaasan in Tokushima, to celebrate Obon (ancestor's remembrance festival). Tokushima is best known for Awa-Odori (a four-day dance festival) that takes place during Obon. The days' buzz with excitement and the nights are filled with the sound of shamisen, grand taiko drums, shinobue flutes, and kane bells. Dance groups, known as ren, meet in empty spaces to practice for the festival. A special chant can be heard: "A Yatto sa," attracting the response, "A Yatto Yatto."

Of all the festivals in Japan, Obon was Yoko's favourite. It brought back happy memories of her childhood and the evenings spent rehearsing for Awa Odori.

Now that she was a mother to a seven-year-old girl, she simply enjoyed the time she got to spend with her mother and daughter. The thought of these festivals made her joyful. Chiharu, on the other hand, was not so happy this Obon. This was due to a wobbly tooth that was causing her great discomfort.

CHAPTER 2

An Unexpected Gift

The lace curtains billowed in the gentle breeze, as the sun peeped through the window and shone on Chiharu's face. It was the morning before Obon. Chiharu peeled her tiny body of her bed and rubbed her eyes. She raised her hand to her mouth and blew a kiss in the air for her late grandfather and father.

She was sure they would receive this loving greeting - especially during Obon. She flopped back onto her bed and stretched to awaken her body. As she did this, she swept past a small object under her pillow. It fell on the floor by her bed.

“Chiharu!” Yoko called from the kitchen. “Breakfast is ready!”

Chiharu brought her feet down and stepped on the small object. She sighed as she made her way to the bathroom.

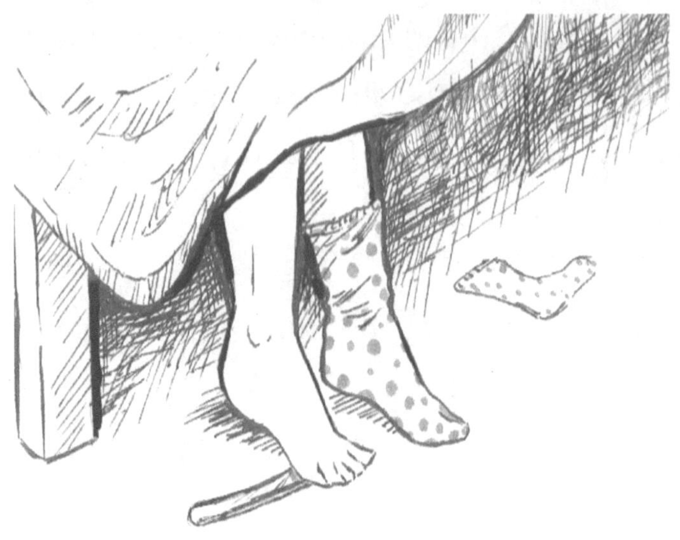

She dragged a small stool to the sink and took a step up. Her tired reflection in the mirror confirmed the need for a few more hours of sleep. She splashed cold water on her face and reached for her toothbrush. As she opened her mouth to brush, she was startled.

She dropped her toothbrush in the sink and rushed back to her bedroom. *Where could it be?* She thought to herself. She sat on her bed and began to sob. By her feet was the object that had left an imprint on the sole of her foot.

“Haru-chan!” Yoko called again. Chiharu picked up the object and ran downstairs, bursting into the kitchen.

“Okaasan!” Chiharu cried. Yoko turned, startled by her entrance.

“What is it?” she asked concernedly.

“My tooth!”

”What about your tooth?”

“It’s gone!”

Yoko remained calm despite Chiharu's unease. She invited her to sit at the table.

"Open your mouth and let me have a look."

Chiharu separated her lips to reveal a missing upper tooth.

Yoko gave a motherly smile.

"My baby's tooth has finally fallen out." She tapped Chiharu playfully on the nose, but Chiharu was unmoved.

"Don't worry dear; it's perfectly normal - it will grow back." Chiharu did not respond to this good news. Yoko knew it would take greater effort to get a smile back on her face. She grabbed a pair of chopsticks from the nearby drawer. As Chiharu sulked, Yoko began to realise that she would have to break with childhood tradition. "Sadly, there will be no throwing of your tooth under the floorboards, but -"

Chiharu huffed and folded her arms in protest. Yoko turned and noticed the small object in Chiharu's hand.

"What's that?" she asked. Chiharu revealed the object. Yoko gasped.

She shifted uncomfortably and took off her apron. She returned to the table and set it ready for breakfast.

“We can’t let the food get cold,” she muttered and took a deep breath. “Itadakimasu.”

“Itadakimasu,” replied Chiharu, to the invitation to eat.

"Okaasan?" Chiharu looked at the presentation of the food on the table. The chopsticks were placed the wrong way. Yoko never did this. Chiharu knew something was wrong. She looked at Yoko questioningly.

"It's just a silly toothbrush!" she quipped.
"Don't say that!" Yoko snapped.
Chiharu recoiled and pulled the small bowl of rice and miso soup towards her.
"Why? What's so special about this toothbrush?"
Yoko shook her head in disbelief.
"During Obon, the spirits of your ancestors come to visit, and that includes the spirit of otousan and ojiisan."
Chiharu smiled as she found the thought comforting.
"If your tooth falls out on the eve of Obon, it means the spirits have taken it away. They replace it with a toothbrush - like this one."

Yoko took the toothbrush and pointed it towards Chiharu's chest.

"The spirits look into your heart through this little gap between your teeth."

Chiharu dabbed her finger on the fleshy part of her gum and pondered.

"Do you know what will happen to your other baby teeth?" Yoko asked.

"They will fall out."

"Yes, and then what?"

"I'll get new teeth."

"Yes, the loss of your tooth is not such a bad thing." Chiharu began to feel better.

"This tiny space will soon be filled with something bigger and better. The spirits have chosen you."

Confusion grew on Chiharu's face as she tried to make sense of it all, she had one burning question.

"- but why do I have this toothbrush?"

Yoko gave a long sigh.

"Why do we brush our teeth?"

Chiharu flopped back on the chair, tired of all the questions being redirected at her.

"Okaasan – tell me, pleeeeease," she whined. "Why do I have this toothbrush?"

Yoko kept quiet and poured herself a glass of green tea. Chiharu was all too familiar with this disciplinary game of silence.

"Ok ... ok ... to get clean, we brush our teeth to get clean."

Defeat crossed Chiharu's face as Yoko delighted in her small win. Yoko went to remove the plates from the dishwasher.

"You must also have a clean heart. You are growing, and you will have to start making wise decisions. The spirits are watching you."

Chiharu examined the toothbrush further. It was small, plain and wooden. It was hard to get excited about such a bland object. She hopped off her chair and headed for the kitchen door. The best place for such an item would be in the bathroom cabinet she thought.

“Where are you going?” Yoko asked.

“To put the toothbrush away.”

Yoko sighed and removed the last plate from the dishwasher.

"How then will you make a wish?"
This shock revelation caused the toothbrush to slip from Chiharu's hand. She scuffled to pick it up. As she rose, so too did the importance of the toothbrush.

"A wish!" she exclaimed.

"Yes ... as I said, this is no ordinary toothbrush. It's a magic toothbrush. It can change into anything you want it to."

Chiharu beamed. Yoko remembered the tempura she had frying on the stove and rushed to lift it from the hot oil.

It was perfectly light and fluffy. She sat it on the kitchen towel to drain and brought it to the table.

“You get five wishes - the only thing is -” she paused.

Chiharu looked at her mother with concern.

“What okaasan?”

Yoko softened her tone.

“You have to make five wishes before the end of Obon ... or .... or ... your tooth might never grow back.”

Chiharu gasped and covered her mouth. Yoko began to feel unsettled.

"Enough now! Eat your food before it gets cold." Yoko served the tempura.

Chiharu reached across the table for another serving of rice and accidentally nudged the chopsticks off the table.

She looked at Yoko embarrassed. She pushed her chair back and stepped down to pick it up; just then, a thought ran through her mind. She popped her head back up.

"Okaasan, how does this toothbrush work?"

It had been many years since Yoko had seen a magic toothbrush. She thought about it for a moment until her thoughts became clear.

“There should be something written on the side of it.”

Chiharu studied the toothbrush. She held it delicately and squinted to read the small print written on the side. As she parted her lips, she hesitated.

“It’s ok,” Yoko said encouragingly.

She took a deep breath and released the magic words from her mouth.

“MAGIC TOOTHBRUSH, DO AS I SAY
TURN INTO [BLANK SPACE] RIGHT AWAY.”

She flipped the toothbrush over and read the rest of the words.

THANK YOU [BLANK SPACE] FOR HELPING ME TODAY,
TURN BACK INTO A TOOTHBRUSH WITHOUT DELAY.

Chiharu took a deep breath and tested the toothbrush's magic qualities.

"Magic toothbrush, do as I say, turn into chopsticks right away." A sudden bout of fear came over Chiharu and she threw the toothbrush on the table. She watched as it transformed into a wooden pair of chopsticks. She gasped. She picked it up with trembling hands and fixed it between her fingers. She ate every grain of rice in her bowl.

Once she had finished, she hopped of her chair and headed towards the kitchen door.

"Chiharu!" Yoko called, "Are you forgetting something?"
Chiharu blushed as she remembered and returned to the chopsticks.

"Thank you, chopsticks, for helping me today. Turn back into a toothbrush without delay." At once, the chopsticks changed back into a toothbrush.

This is going to be easy, Chiharu thought to herself.

CHAPTER 3
Thirst

Yoko placed their cases in the boot of her car and did a quick check of the car's oil and water level before setting off for Tokushima.
"Did you turn off the lights?"
"Yes okaasan."
"Shut all the windows?"
"Yes okaasan."
"Remove the plates from the dishwasher?"
Chiharu entered into the game of silence. Upon realising, Yoko laughed.
"Ok, let's go!"

The journey to Tokushima was long and tiring. Chiharu stared out the window, thinking about all the things she could possibly wish for with the magic toothbrush.

This was the first time that Chiharu was allowed to sit at the front of the car. It was also Yoko's first time driving to Tokushima without her husband. Neither of them let on about just how nervous they really were.

"Are we there yet," Chiharu asked every so often.

"Almost," Yoko replied every time.

"Maybe I can use my toothbrush to get us there faster."

"Try to sit back and enjoy the journey." Yoko laughed as she noticed just how much she sounded like her late husband.

"But I want to see obaachan now," Chiharu whined. Her voice began to fade as Yoko drifted off into a daydream.

"Okaasan . . . okaasan," Chiharu called. The sound of the honking horns soon ended Yoko's escape from reality.

"The lights have changed."

Yoko pulled herself together and released her foot off the brakes.

"Okaasan, are you okay?" Chiharu asked.

"Yes," Yoko replied, sweeping her hair behind her ears. "I was just thinking back to this time last year."

Chiharu looked at her mother questioningly. She unzipped her bag and searched for the magic toothbrush. As she rehearsed the magic words in her head, she was met by the word *patience;* an attitude encouraged by her father. She stopped and released the toothbrush from her hand. She zipped up her bag, stared out the window and smiled.

Yoko and Chiharu arrived at obaasan's house in time for lunch. She had made ohagi, sweet rice cake with red beans; this was Chiharu's favourite treat.

As they ate, Chiharu told obaasan about the toothbrush.

“Use it sensibly,” she advised.

After lunch, Yoko gave obaasan her presents. She was extremely pleased. Gardening tools were always a welcomed gift. Obaasan used the time to show Yoko and Chiharu around her garden. It was lush and well kept. She was extremely proud of it. She had designed a separate area for the fruits and vegetables. Yoko and Chiharu praised her for her efforts.

As they admired her garden, the sun beamed down on them. The heat became too much for Chiharu and made her feel thirsty. Rather than go indoors for a jug of freshly squeezed juice, she decided to make a second wish.

“Magic toothbrush, do as I say, turn into a glass of water right away.”

Immediately, the toothbrush changed into a glass of water. Chiharu gulped it down and let out a satisfying sigh before uttering the magic words.

“Thank you glass of water for helping me today, turn back into a toothbrush without delay.”

Immediately, the glass changed back into the toothbrush, but unexpectedly - Chiharu's thirst returned. Beads of sweat began to collect on her forehead. She rubbed her chin, confused. She dragged her feet along to the stone steps and buried her head between her folded arms.

She remembered obaasan's advice.

U*se it sensibly!*

CHAPTER 4
The Secret's Out!

The sun poured through the window and brought light into the room. It was the first day of Obon. Chiharu blew a kiss towards the window and jumped out of bed feeling a lot more hopeful for the day. The sound of laughter could be heard from the kitchen. She skipped along the hallway to the kitchen and sat down besides Yoko at the dinner table.

"Ohayou!"

"Ohayou!" they said, greeting each other good morning.

"What's so funny?" Chiharu asked.

Obaasan brought over three bowls of natto and took a seat at the table.

"Itadakimasu," she bid.

"Itadakimasu" they replied.

Chiharu's face dropped as she stared at the strong-smelling soya beans in her bowl. She began to swirl her chopsticks around the food.

"Is anything wrong dear?" obaasan asked concernedly.

"No," replied Chiharu glumly.

Obaasan turned to Yoko, who then covered her mouth and looked the other way.

Chiharu stopped playing with her food and rested the chopsticks by the side of the bowl. She looked at the door, longing for her father to come in and save her. He would distract everyone by asking them to share their plans for the day, whilst signalling to Chiharu to scoop her serving of natto into his bowl. But this year, sadly, he wasn't there to do that.

"I forgot something." Chiharu pushed her chair back and headed for the kitchen door. Yoko and obaasan erupted with laughter. Chiharu turned to look at what was going on.

"What's so funny?" she asked.

“Darling, we know,” replied Yoko.

“Know what?”

“That you don’t like natto. We were just wondering how long you were going to keep this secret from us.”

Chiharu paused and then burst into tears as the shame set in.

“Your mother never liked natto either when she was your age,” obaasan added.

“I still don’t,” Yoko laughed.

“It’s not funny!”

Chiharu sobbed.

Yoko gestured for Chiharu to sit on her lap and dried her tears.

“It might not taste nice, but it’s good for you,” she said.

Chiharu broke a faint smile.

“How did you know?” Chiharu asked.

“A mother always knows,” they replied in one voice.

Though embarrassed, Chiharu was glad that she had escaped the yucky mush in her bowl – however healthy they claimed it to be. Yoko kissed her forehead, as obaasan brought over a bowl of miso soup instead.

CHAPTER 5

Onsen

After breakfast, Yoko, obaasan and Chiharu packed a bag and headed to the hot springs. As they approached, it began to rain heavily. They waited in the car park for the rain to stop, but it continued, battering the exterior of the car.

Chiharu grew impatient and thought of an idea. She padded the pockets of her jacket and pulled out the magic toothbrush.

"Magic toothbrush, do as I say, turn into an umbrella right away."

Immediately, the toothbrush changed into an umbrella – a small umbrella. They huddled up close together and made their way to the hot spring.

Once inside, Chiharu placed the umbrella in an umbrella stand to dry. Obaasan and Yoko praised her for being so thoughtful and headed to the changing room.

The hot spring was the perfect way to unwind. It had many baths with various minerals, all of which were good for the body. Chiharu enjoyed the hydrogen bath because of the tiny bubbles it produced. She liked the feeling of the silk against her skin. Obaasan spent most of her time in the sulphur bath, as it brought light relief to her painful knees. She lay back relaxed with her arms spread out and a small damp towel over her head. Yoko liked the sauna and steam room the most. After a few minutes, she would dip herself in a cold bath. Chiharu winced every time she did this.

After some time, they returned to the changing room to get ready to go home. Obaasan had planned to visit ojiisan's grave later that day. On the way home, Chiharu fidgeted around in her bag for the magic toothbrush.

"Wait!" she shouted.

Yoko slammed her foot on the brakes. They returned to the hot springs and made their way to the umbrella stand. It was now full of umbrellas.

"Oh no!" Chiharu cried, "It's impossible. I don't know which one is mine. They all look the same."

Chiharu picked up the umbrella closest to her and said the magic words, but nothing happened. She picked up a few more, but none of them changed into the toothbrush.

"I hate this stupid toothbrush," she cried.

Yoko put her arms around her to offer comfort.

"It's here somewhere; we just need to find it."

A visitor passed and picked up an umbrella. Chiharu looked on in despair, too beaten by fate to say anything. A tear rolled down her cheek.

"I want to go home now," she sobbed.

"How many wishes do you have left?" asked Yoko.

"Two."

"Then we must find it."

One by one, Chiharu picked up the black umbrellas and said the magic words. When she got to the last umbrella, she had lost all hope.

“Thank you toothbrush for helping me today, turn back into an umbrella without delay.” NOTHING!

"Oh darling don't worry, we'll speak to the receptionist and see if maybe -" just then, there was a clanking sound by the umbrella stand. There lay the magic toothbrush. Chiharu pressed her palm to her heart and exhaled. She picked it up and placed it safely in her pocket. They headed home in silence.

CHAPTER 6
Koen

Once home, Yoko removed the wet towels from the bags as Chiharu moped around the house. She stared out the window at the rens rehearsing for Awa Odori, but couldn't bring herself to get excited about the festival. Yoko tried to cheer her up, but it was all in vain. After a while, she asked if she could go to the park. Seeing how upset she had been earlier, Yoko agreed.

"Make sure you're back by 6 -"
Chiharu rushed out the door before Yoko could finish her sentence.

The children's playground was fairly basic. It had just a few apparatuses, but the children enjoyed it all the same. Chiharu looked around and spotted a few children she felt she could make friends with.

She swung high on the swings and slid down the slides. She made a friend on the see-saw and said her goodbyes. She joined another group of children by the climbing frame and gave up halfway on the monkey bars. She tried again. She ran around, she stopped and ran around some more. Time passed by quickly. She rolled up her sleeve to check the time.

“Oh no!” she cried as she stared at her bare wrist. She panicked. She asked a few of the children if they knew the time, but nobody could help. It was getting late. She reached for the magic toothbrush. She thought for a moment, then proceeded with the magic words.

"Magic toothbrush, do as I say, turn into a watch right away."

Immediately, the toothbrush transformed into a watch. Chiharu huffed as she looked at her wasted wish. This was not what she had expected. What a disaster. It was nothing like the digital watch she owned. She steadied herself. *I can do this.* She began to count the seconds on the watch, but it was no use. She could not read the time. She dropped her head and hands down, disappointed. Just then, a group of children sped past her on their bikes. She stepped out of the way.

A thought drifted into her mind, but with just one wish left, she snapped out of it and built up enough determination and speed to run home.

Yoko was waiting outside the house by the garden entrance.

"I was a little worried. I found your watch in my bag when you left for the park."

Chiharu stood hunched over the gate, trying to catch her breath.

"I took it off at the onsen," she responded breathlessly. "I didn't want to get it wet -"

Yoko smiled. "My smart little girl, the spirits would be proud."

Chiharu rolled down her sleeves discreetly and gave a half-hearted smile.

"Shall I help you put it on?"

"Oh no, that's ok, I can do it myself," Chiharu replied. She glanced over to the garden.

"What's obaasan doing?"

"She's picking flowers to take to ojiisan's grave."

Chiharu smiled and began to make her way indoors.

"Chiharu!" Yoko called.

Chiharu slowed down. Her eyes grew wide.

"Yes okaasan?" She waited for Yoko to continue speaking, but not a word came out.

She turned, with a nervous smile. *She knows about the watch,* she thought to herself.
"Don't forget," Yoko glanced over at obaasan to make sure she wasn't listening. She continued in a low voice. "Tomorrow is obaasan's birthday."

Chiharu breathed a sigh of relief and made her way into the dining room. In the corner of the room was a shrine for family members that had passed away. She stopped at it, clasped her hands together and bowed her head. She thought about Yoko's words. *Would the spirits really be proud?* She sighed. She replaced the watches and reversed the spell. Beneath the shrine was a drawer. She opened it and took out a sheet of paper and some crayons.

In the early evening, they took a stroll to the cemetery to visit ojiisan's grave. Obaasan ran water into a bucket and cleaned his stone. She lay down the flowers and placed incense sticks in the pots beside it. Chiharu missed her grandfather very much. She remembered all the fun they had together, going for long walks and taking pictures of nature.

“Obaasan, can we climb up the mountain?” Chiharu asked.

“My knees won’t allow it,” obaasan sighed.

“But obasaan, it’ll be fun.”

They agreed to climb the next day.

CHAPTER 7
Enjoy The Moment

It was an unusually windy day, but Chiharu, Yoko and obaasan were determined to trek to the top of the mountain.

On a good day, it would take just under an hour. This time, it took a little longer. Chiharu remembered the many journeys she made with her late father and grandfather. It brought back happy and sad memories.

"Don't go too far," ojiisan would call out before she disappeared into the distance. He would then grab his chest as she jumped out to scare him. When she got tired, she would jump on otousan's back and listen to their conversations about sports, politics or work. This time around the journey was a little different. This was the first journey they made without otousan and ojiisan.

Chiharu thought back to all the times she asked whether they had reached the top of the mountain yet.

"Try to enjoy the journey; it's better than the endpoint," otousan would reply every time. Chiharu began to make sense of his words. She slowed down and waited for Yoko and obaasan. When they reached the top, they praised each other for their efforts. Chiharu looked around at her surroundings, as she turned left, she recognised where they were and ran ahead.

"Come! Come!" she beckoned from a spot that offered the best view of Tokushima. Yoko and obaasan increased their pace. When they reached, they marvelled at the landscape.

"This is amazing," they remarked. Chiharu smiled, pleased that she had convinced them to climb the mountain. She wedged her way between them and held their hands.

"Did you like the journey?" she asked.

Obaasan nodded.

"What about you okaasan?"

"I sure did darling, and you?" Chiharu thought for a brief moment.

"I'm not quite sure... otousan always said the journey was better than the endpoint but-"

"Yes?" Yoko enquired.

"I'm glad it's over."

They laughed.

"Look!" Obaasan pointed to familiar landmarks.

"There's Yoshino river . . . there's the boardwalk . . . there's the clock tower . . . there's the new bridge."

"This was Ojiisan's favourite spot." Chiharu pondered with a tinge of sadness.

They remained silent and took in the beautiful scenery. Chiharu made a suggestion.

"Why don't we take a picture?"

"That's a lovely idea, but no one has brought a camera. Let's just enjoy the moment," Yoko replied.

Chiharu released her hand from their hand and protested.

"Remember ojiisan's words, it's more important to enjoy the moment than to photograph it, and he himself was a photographer."

Chiharu huffed. "I know, but I have one wish left."

"Are you sure you want to use your last wish?" Yoko asked.

"Yes, I'm sure."

Yoko smiled and patted Chiharu on the shoulder. Chiharu took out the toothbrush and thought one last time.

"Magic toothbrush, do as I say, turn into a camera right away."

Immediately, the toothbrush changed into a camera. Chiharu sighed as she looked at the old fashioned Polaroid camera before her. It was similar to the one her grandfather used to use. This was not what she had expected. It was too late now, she shrugged. She looked around and asked a passer-by to take their photograph.

They huddled up close together and smiled into the lens of the camera. The wind rattled the trees. The flash went off, and an instant film ejected slowly from the front. Chiharu remembered what her grandfather used to do with the film and waved it from side to side.

"What are you doing ojiisan?" Chiharu asked the first time she saw him do this. Ojiisan smiled.

"Some people think it helps the film develop faster...that's nonsense, everything happens at the right time. I just do this to pass the time."

A gust of wind swept the film out of Chiharu's hand. She followed it with her eyes. It landed on a drinks machine. She ran to it and peeled it off. As she stared at the bottles of water in the machine, her face dropped.
She remembered what had happened in obaasan's garden with the glass of water. *What would happen to the film when she reversed the spell?*

She despaired. *What if the photograph disappeared like the water did?*

Chiharu's eyes began to fill with tears as she watched the film develop into a beautiful family portrait. Yoko and obaasan noticed how upset she was and went over to comfort her.

Obaasan wrapped her arms around Chiharu and rocked her gently. Yoko looked in her handbag for a handkerchief to dry Chiharu's eyes.

"It was very thoughtful of you darling." As much as they tried to raise her spirits, they knew it was no good. Yoko put the camera in her bag and brought out the birthday card that Chiharu had made for her the day before. She wished her a happy birthday, but her heart was broken.

“Probably best not to reverse the spell just yet”, Yoko advised. They made their way back down the mountain using the cable cart instead.

When they arrived home, obaasan put the photograph inside the birthday card, and placed it in the glass cabinet along with the camera.

“It’s almost time for bed now, why don’t you go and have your bath,” Yoko said.

Chiharu sat in the bath sobbing. She thought about her difficult few days. As the water in the tub cooled, she knew it was time to get out and go to bed.

The sound of musical instruments radiated in the air. “A yatto sa, A yatto sa,” rens bellowed. Chiharu looked out the window at the many people making their way to Awa Odori.

“Here you are!” Chiharu turned to see Yoko standing by the door in a brand new yukata and one laid out on her bed. Chiharu smiled.

“Put this on, we’re going to Awa Odori.” Yoko raised her arms gracefully, ready for her best dance performance. She alternated them, sweeping the air with her hands. She raised her knees in the opposite direction, balancing on her wooden Geta sandals.

“A yatto sa, a yatto sa!” They chanted merrily.

"Yatto Yatto," obaasan replied. They turned. Obaasan strolled into the bedroom also wearing a new Yukata.

"What do you think of my birthday present?" Chiharu smiled as she recognised the gift.

Once ready, they followed behind the many people making their way to the festival.

Yoko and Chiharu danced with the rens till late in the evening. Obaasan stood back and watched. They wandered around the food stalls and street vendors. They took their seats and watched a special show that showcased all the different rens. That night Chiharu went to bed with her heart full, buzzing with excitement.

CHAPTER 8

The Moment Of Truth

The following morning, Chiharu woke to the buzzing of cicadas. Her heart sank as she remembered the camera. She ran into obaasan's bedroom, forgetting to perform her morning ritual. Yoko was already up. They made their way to the living room. The card appeared to still be in the glass cabinet, but the camera was nowhere to be seen. Obaasan opened the cabinet and removed the card, out fell the film - it was blank.

As Yoko knelt to pick it up, her hand gave way.

She paused, composed herself, and tried again.

She flipped the film over. There was silence. They gasped. There before them was a glossy family portrait set at the top of the mountain. Upon studying the image closer, there appeared to be two men that looked like ojiisan and otousan, but they couldn't be sure. They wept with joy.

Obaasan stood by the car and bid her daughter and granddaughter goodbye.

“I’m so proud of you Haru-chan, I wish your mother and I were as wise as you when we were your age.” She turned to Yoko and winked. They set off for Nagoya.

Chiharu recalled everything that had happened over the past few days. She occasionally looked at her watch to see how many minutes had passed since the last time she looked.

“Try to enjoy the-”

“I know... I know,” Chiharu replied smugly. They laughed. Chiharu stared adoringly at the photograph.

Chiharu missed having the magic toothbrush, but she was happy that the spirits of the past had trusted her to make some of the most important decisions of her life. This was one Obon, Chiharu would never forget.

The End.

BACKGROUND

I left London for Japan in 2011 to work as an English conversation teacher. This was the same year that Japan had experienced the Fukushima Daiichi nuclear disaster. Not everyone understood my reasons for wanting to go. However, I had made up my mind. The optimism I had built up slowly evaporated as I sat waiting at Nagoya Chubu Airport for the company director to pick me up. We'd discussed my flight details over email, so why hadn't he come to get me- *had I been duped.* My fears began to fade, following a phone call to head office. They confirmed that someone was indeed on their way to get me. That evening, as I lay my jet-lagged body on a futon mattress, on the hard floor, I questioned my migratory decision, whilst listening to overzealous twenty-something-year-olds ramble on about being in Japan. It comforted me to know that I was in Nagoya for just a few days to train as a Native teacher.

As I stood outside Tokushima station for the first time, the realisation hit me that this was going to be home for at least a year. I was already drawing comparisons to my hometown Brixton. The station was close by and the art was warm and welcoming.

Outside Tokushima station, Japan

Stockwell Park Walk (Brixton) London

Once in Tokushima, I was assigned to three schools in Yoshinogawa, Komatsushima and Matsushige.

I drew inspiration for this book from several sources and experiences. After finishing work at Matsushige, I would pass a billboard that showed a young girl flying on a toothbrush, *how wonderfully bizarre* I thought to myself, but so were a lot of things in Japan, such as the ability to grab a canned hot chocolate or tea from a vending machine.

The main character in this story is called Chiharu. There is no particular reason why I chose this name, other than that I taught two students with the same name. It's a beautiful sounding Japanese name, and its three syllables make it that more impactful. I wanted it to be apparent whenever someone picked up this book that we were going on a journey to Japan.

A part of teaching that I later came to appreciate was in my lessons with the older students. In these lessons, the students would be given a short extract about traditional festivals and holidays - such as Hinamatsuri, Setsuban, and Obon. What I gained from this, was a basic understanding of festivals and the culture, what's more, I was able to participate and experience these events for myself.

I was incredibly blessed to meet some phenomenal people whilst living in Japan. Through them, I was afforded an authentic Japanese experience. I joined Tokushima Christian Reformed Church and was involved in their children's ministry - Happy Kids. The Terauchi family were a God-send, and Miwa Numata-san always made sure that whenever there was an opportunity to experience something *Japanesy* (as I would say), I would be part of it. Through her, I met Kimiko Matsumura-san, a wonderful garden designer, incredibly knowledgeable in her field; the garden scene in the story was a nod to her.

I took on a casual job at T Place, a talking café, where I sat and talked with local Japanese visitors about every and anything - mostly current affairs. Thank you Tony Masuya-san for having the vision to set up such an inclusive establishment where one can learn from and about each other. There I met the merry Kelekolio Maka- san his wife Mary Maka-san and their wonderful children. I met Yoko-san (respectfully) an unassuming warm-hearted lady with a heart of gold. We had many memorable conversations whilst dining at either a quaint, Eurocentric, or traditional restaurant in Tokushima. Sadly, we lost contact, but I often get a sense of natsukashi (nostalgia) when I revisit my photographs.

Another blessing came in the form of the Fushitani family. I built a wonderful friendship with Kana-san, her husband Akira-san and children Yuka and Ryotaro Fushitani. I always felt like part of the family. The experiences we shared were invaluable, and Kana-san's aura was always so peaceful and contented.

No gaijin (foreigner) could live in Tokushima without visiting Bourbon Street Music Bar, a mellow jazz place. One could always expect a warm welcome from Vivian Hernaez-san, and for those with a bit more verve – the place to be was Ingrid's Bar for a tad of karaoke and dancing till the early hours. Ingrid Hashimoto-san has touched so many different lives.

I worked along with some fantastic and committed teachers in Tokushima - Kana Thomason-san, whose enthusiasm and energy for teaching was unmatched.

One of my biggest regrets about living in Japan was not being wholly present in the moment. There are elements of this embedded in the story.

Being present is a work in progress, the here and now is the greatest gift. If I never speak of Japan again - I am content knowing that I've finally published this book.

OTHER BOOKS BY JOANA JEHU APPIAH:

Elijah: Journeying Through a Pandemic

Akwasi Has Arrived

www.ingramcontent.com/pod-product-compliance
Lightning Source LLC
LaVergne TN
LVHW051017080826
845145LV00009B/2677